For Willow with lots of love. — K.S

First published in 2015 by Enchanted Lion Books,
351 Van Brunt Street, Brooklyn, NY 11231

Original Norwegian edition published by Det Norske Samlaget, Norway,
as *Historia Om Korleis Hunden Fekk Våt Snute*
Copyright © Det Norske Samlaget, 2012
Published by Agreement with Hagen Agency, Norway
Copyright © 2015 by Kenneth Steven for the English-language text

ISBN 978-1-59270-173-5

A CIP record is on file with the Library of Congress

Printed by South China Printing Company

First Printing

WHY DOGS HAVE WET NOSES

ENCHANTED LION BOOKS
NEW YORK

A long, long time ago, not long after the world began, it started to rain. It was the kind of rain that really soaks you, pouring down from the sky like it will never stop.

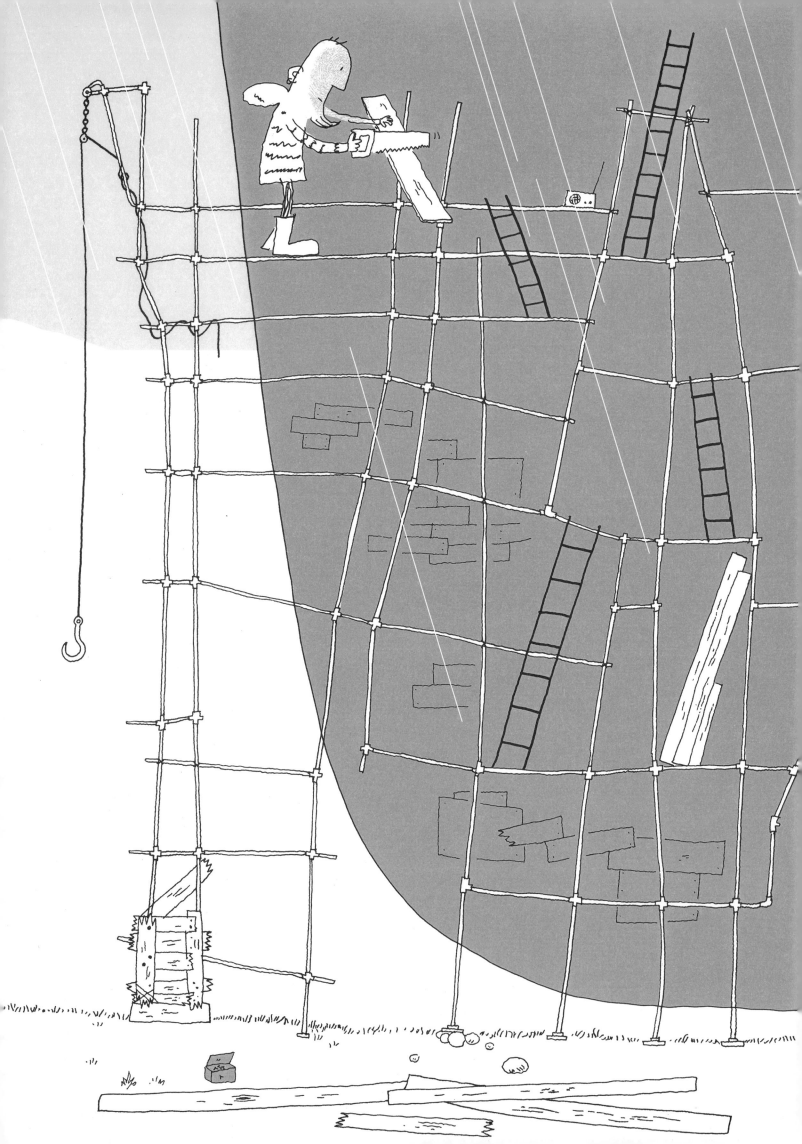

At this same time, there lived a man named Noah, who was both watchful and wise. So it was that as the clouds gathered overhead and the storm rumbled, he began to build a lifeboat. He used enormous trees to make it and called it — the Ark.

CAFÉ

Noah went far and wide to gather together as many creatures as he could remember. He even invited slugs, spiders, and other creepy-crawlies — bugs that most people get rid of by stomping on them with their foot or squishing them with their thumb — onto the Ark.

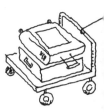

Last of all, a dog padded on board. He was such a funny mixture that it was hard to tell what exactly he was, but there could be no doubt about his dog's nose, which was soft and black.

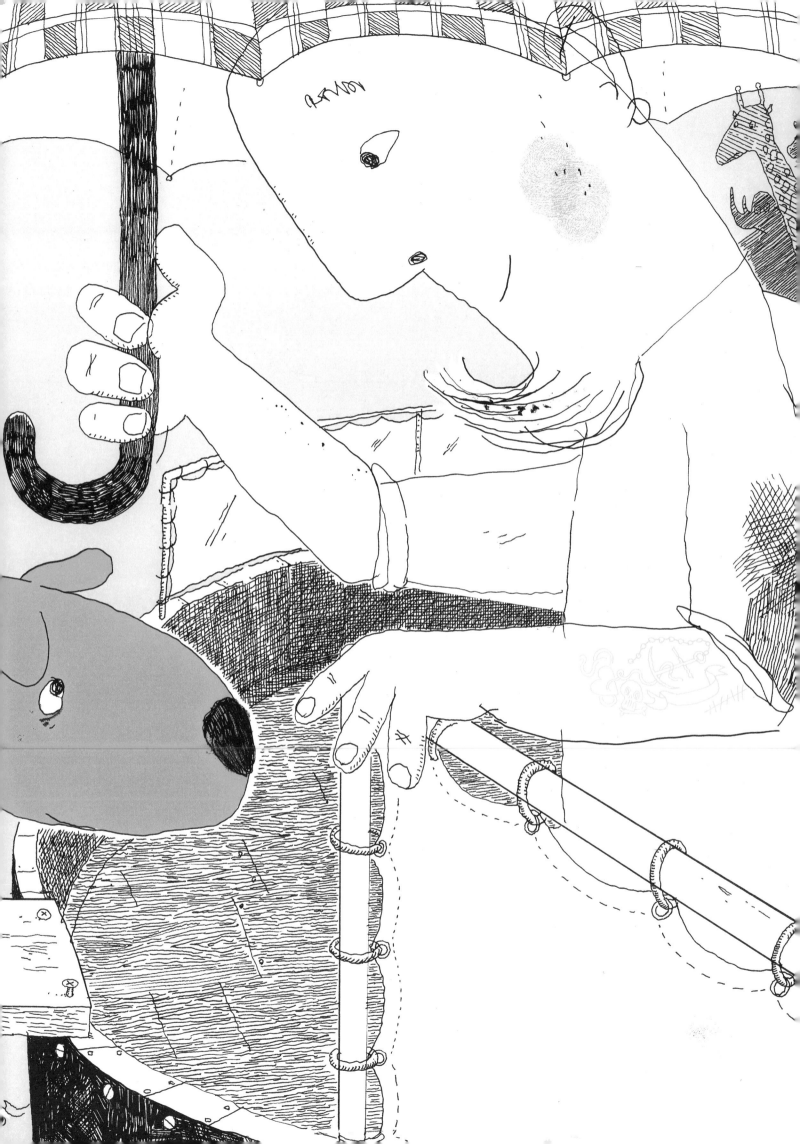

Noah invited so many animals on board that the Ark gave a great groan and tilted to one side. Noah held his breath, afraid that the boat was so big and so heavy that it would never float. They waited as the rain poured down and the waters rose. At last, a mighty wave rolled towards them, lifting the lifeboat. Despite its great weight, the Ark floated. Their voyage into the unknown had begun.

They sailed away. Land had long since vanished. Only sea and sky remained. The rain fell heavier and heavier, and lightning shot from the black clouds, gleaming like snakes' tongues. But apart from the crashing sounds of rain and thunder, it was completely quiet. As though there were no other sounds left in the whole wide world.

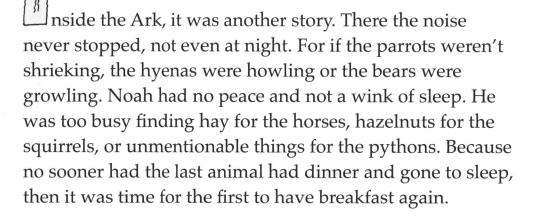

nside the Ark, it was another story. There the noise never stopped, not even at night. For if the parrots weren't shrieking, the hyenas were howling or the bears were growling. Noah had no peace and not a wink of sleep. He was too busy finding hay for the horses, hazelnuts for the squirrels, or unmentionable things for the pythons. Because no sooner had the last animal had dinner and gone to sleep, then it was time for the first to have breakfast again.

After they'd been out on the ocean for twenty days, something terrible happened. The Ark sprang a leak! It came from a hole no bigger than a chestnut. Not much in a boat the size of a football field. But before Noah had time to shout for help, there was water everywhere and a rabbit had to be rescued. "What in the world are we going to do?" Noah said to his dog. They needed a plan — fast!

POTATO
CHIP

The monkeys shrieked, the donkeys brayed, the mice clapped their little paws, and Noah and his wife danced for joy. The Ark had been saved!

The rain fell for forty days and forty nights, and the ocean stretched as far as the eye could see. But since Noah's dog loved his master, he stayed completely still, with his nose in the hole. Night and day, the water washed up over his nose, but not a single drop came into the Ark. Then one early morning, the dog caught the scent of something else.

and! Hills rose up through the mist, and behind them there was a tiny bit of blue sky. The rain had stopped at last and a magnificent rainbow stretched across the sky.

They'd reached land! And what a beautiful sight it was!
Once more, all kinds of things were growing upon the
earth.

oah gently stroked his dog's tummy.

"Good boy," he whispered.

"Woof!" the dog replied, leaping up to give his master a kiss with his wet nose.

Never again would Noah's dog have to go to sea. But from then on, every dog in the world would have a wet nose.